THE TWELVE DAYS OF CHRISTMAS

In memory of my father, Don
J.R.

ORCHARD BOOKS
338 Euston Road, London NW1 3BH
Orchard Books Australia
Level 17/207 Kent Street, Sydney, NSW 2000

First published in 2011 by Orchard Books

ISBN 978 1 40830 703 8

Illustrations © Jane Ray 2011

The right of Jane Ray to be identified as the illustrator of
this book has been asserted by her in accordance with the
Copyright, Designs and Patents Act, 1988.

A CIP catalogue record for this book is available from
the British Library.

1 3 5 7 9 10 8 6 4 2

Printed in China

Orchard Books is a division of Hachette Children's Books,
an Hachette UK company.
www.hachette.co.uk

THE TWELVE DAYS OF
CHRISTMAS

To~
My True Love
x

Jane Ray

ORCHARD BOOKS

On the first day of Christmas,
my true love sent to me
A partridge in a pear tree.

On the second day of Christmas,
my true love sent to me
Two turtle doves,
And a partridge in a pear tree.

On the third day of Christmas,
  my true love sent to me
Three French hens,
Two turtle doves,
And a partridge in a pear tree.

On the fourth day of Christmas,
my true love sent to me
Four calling birds,
Three French hens,
Two turtle doves,
And a partridge in a pear tree.

On the fifth day of Christmas,
my true love sent to me
Five golden rings . . .

Four calling birds,
Three French hens,
Two turtle doves,
And a partridge in a pear tree.

On the sixth day of Christmas,
  my true love sent to me
Six geese a-laying,
Five golden rings,
Four calling birds,
Three French hens,
Two turtle doves,
And a partridge in a pear tree.

On the seventh day of Christmas,
  my true love sent to me
Seven swans a-swimming,
Six geese a-laying,
Five golden rings,
Four calling birds,
Three French hens,
Two turtle doves,
And a partridge in a pear tree.

On the eighth day of Christmas,
my true love sent to me
Eight maids a-milking,
Seven swans a-swimming,
Six geese a-laying,
Five golden rings,
Four calling birds,
Three French hens,
Two turtle doves,
And a partridge in a pear tree.

On the ninth day of Christmas,
　my true love sent to me
Nine ladies dancing,
Eight maids a-milking,
Seven swans a-swimming,
Six geese a-laying,
Five golden rings,
Four calling birds,
Three French hens,
Two turtle doves,
And a partridge in a pear tree.

On the tenth day of Christmas,
    my true love sent to me
Ten lords a-leaping,
Nine ladies dancing,
Eight maids a-milking,
Seven swans a-swimming,

Six geese a-laying,
Five golden rings,
Four calling birds,
Three French hens,
Two turtle doves,
And a partridge in a pear tree.

On the eleventh day of Christmas,
  my true love sent to me
Eleven pipers piping,
Ten lords a-leaping,
Nine ladies dancing,
Eight maids a-milking,
Seven swans a-swimming,

Six geese a-laying,
Five golden rings,
Four calling birds,
Three French hens,
Two turtle doves,
And a partridge in a pear tree.

On the twelfth day of Christmas,
my true love sent to me
Twelve drummers drumming,
Eleven pipers piping,
Ten lords a-leaping,
Nine ladies dancing . . .

Eight maids a-milking,
Seven swans a-swimming,
Six geese a-laying,
Five golden rings,
Four calling birds,
Three French hens,
Two turtle doves . . .

And a partridge in a pear tree!